Where Does My Cat Sleep?

Norma Simon *pictures* *by* Dora Leder

ALBERT WHITMAN & COMPANY, NILES, ILLINOIS

Library of Congress Cataloging in Publication Data

Simon, Norma.
    Where does my cat sleep?

    Summary: At night each member of the family sleeps
in his or her own bed, but Rocky the cat sleeps anywhere
and everywhere.
    [1. Cats—Fiction. 2. Night—Fiction.
3. Sleep—Fiction] I. Leder, Dora, ill. II. Title.
PZ7.S6053Wi 1982   [E]   82-10872
ISBN 0-8075-8926-8

The text of this book is set in sixteen point Fairfield.

Text © 1982 by Norma Simon
Illustrations © 1982 by Dora Leder
Published in 1982 by Albert Whitman & Company, Niles, Illinois
Published simultaneously in Canada by General Publishing, Limited, Toronto
All rights reserved. Printed in the United States of America.
Second Printing 1983.
10   9   8   7   6   5   4   3

Where do I sleep?
In my bed,
with my panda.

I go to sleep there
every night.
I wake up there
every morning.

But my cat is something else.
Do you know where Rocky sleeps?

On top of cabinets,
way up high.

In dresser drawers,
between the socks.

He sleeps on chairs—

this chair,

this chair,

or this chair.

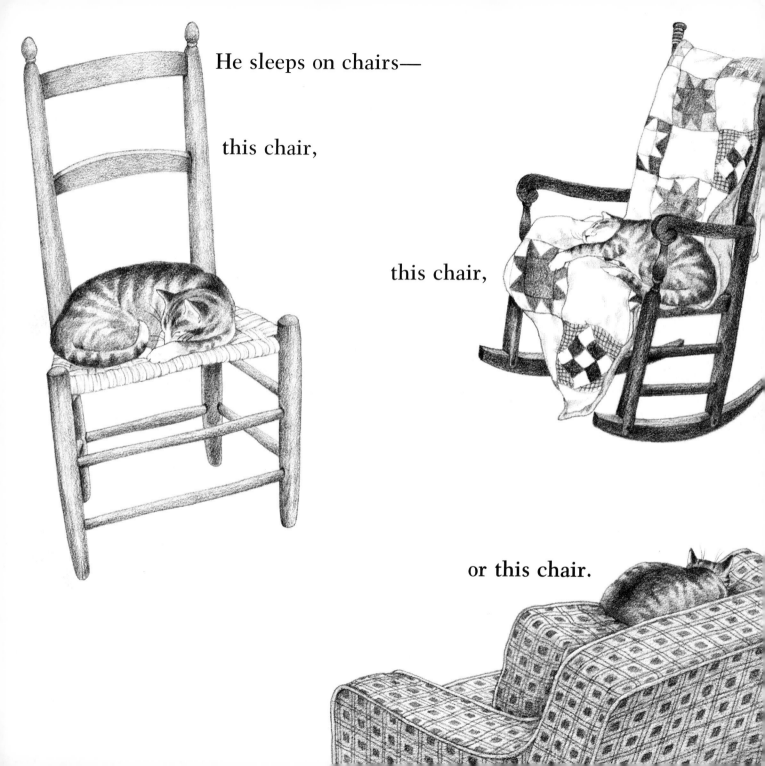

He sleeps halfway
   down the stairs,
  on the rug
   when the sun shines there.

Where does our baby sleep?
In her crib.
Cozy,
cuddly,
sleepy
baby.
Baby sleeps a lot.

My cat likes to sleep on my bed,
but he *can't* sleep in baby's crib.
Mommy said so.

Rocky doesn't care.
He sleeps on top of rags
in the laundry basket,

or in the sink.

He falls asleep inside paper bags
and empty boxes.

Where do Mommy and Daddy sleep?
Together
   in their big bed,
   under big covers,
   in a big bedroom.

When I wake them up
   too early in the morning,
   they grumble and groan.
They want to sleep some more
   and I let them.

My cat likes to sleep
　　on Mommy and Daddy's bed
　　or in our old cradle
　　or in my sleeping bag.

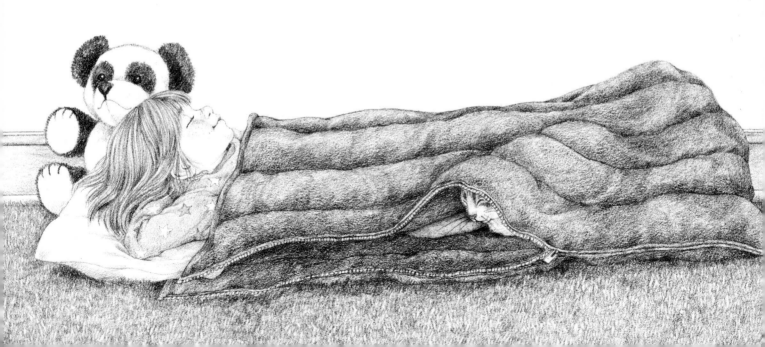

He falls asleep on my lap
when I watch TV.
(He wakes up for
cat food commercials.)

Where does Grandpa sleep?
  In his room,
  in his bed.
He has a big bed
  with a deer carved on the back.
Sometimes I sit on Grandpa's bed
  when he reads me a story.

After lunch, Grandpa sleeps in his chair.
Some days Rocky takes a nap on Grandpa's lap.
He likes to be near Grandpa.
Grandpa pets him a lot.

Everyone has a special place to sleep.
But not my cat.

He sleeps upstairs,

he sleeps downstairs.

When he wakes up he purrs
    and cuddles
    and stretches.
He scratches himself
    and licks himself
    and then he sleeps some more.

He sleeps indoors,

he sleeps outdoors.

He sleeps under things

and inside things.

I don't know where *your* cat sleeps,
but *my* cat sleeps

anywhere he wants.